Charles Townsend

The doctor

An original comic drama in three acts

Charles Townsend

The doctor
An original comic drama in three acts

ISBN/EAN: 9783337303754

Printed in Europe, USA, Canada, Australia, Japan

Cover: Foto ©Andreas Hilbeck / pixelio.de

More available books at **www.hansebooks.com**

THE DOCTOR

An Original Comic Drama in Three Acts

BY

CHARLES TOWNSEND

Author of "Rio Grande," "The Spy of Gettysburg," "Finnigan's Fortune,"
"The Mountain Waif," "The Vagabonds," "Moses," etc.

AUTHOR'S EDITION

BOSTON

1897

THE DOCTOR.

CHARACTERS.

DILLINGTON HOPPER, *a New York stockbroker, who wants some* **fun—** *and gets it.*

THOMAS PICTON, *his friend, who wants peace—and* **doesn't get it.**

CRUMLEY CHUGGS, *a* **nice** *old man, who wants the* **widow—and** *gets her.*

NAPOLEON B. PLUNKER, *an inventor, who wants* **the earth—a**nd *keeps* **on** *wanting.*

MRS. FANNY MAYFAIR, *a dashing young widow, who* **wants a "lark"—** *and has* **it.**

MRS. ANASTASIA BILLOWBY, *another widow,* **who wants to** *elope—and* **is** *disappointed.*

EFFIE PICTON, *Tom's wife, who* **wants revenge—and then** *there's trouble.*

TIME.—Midsummer. PLACE.—ACTS I. and III., Tom's country home.
ACT II., a woodland glade.

Time of playing, two hours and fifteen minutes.

COSTUMES.

(*See*, also, *Remarks on the Play*.)

HOPPER.—*Act I.*—Light sack suit, low shoes, derby or straw hat, fancy shirt, windsor tie. *Act II.*—Regulation outing suit except that, as he is out shooting, he wears leggins, and carries a gun and game-bag. The suit should be of dark gray or blue flannel. A straw hat or cap may be worn. *Act III.*—Evening dress.

TOM.—*Act I.*—Usual summer suit. *Act II.*—Customary outing suit to contrast with Hopper's. *Act III.*—Evening dress.

PLUNKER.—*Act I.*—Loud suit of check material with broad striped trousers. Fancy shirt, flaming tie and a profusion of jewelry. *Act II.*—Gaudy outing suit, with duplicate badly torn for second entrance. *Act III.*—First suit: Same as last, the rents being pinned up. Second suit: Evening dress, but in bad taste; fancy vest, large diamond studs and rings—but be careful to avoid carrying this to the point of burlesque.

CHUGGS.—Ministerial style—plain black throughout. Torn suit for change in Second Act. In Act Third change to evening dress.

FANNY.—*Act I.*—Riding habit in black or olive green. Gloves, whip. *Act II.*—Elegant outing suit. *Act III.*—Same as Act Second, change to evening dress.

MRS. BILLOWBY.—*Act I.*—Very rich tea gown or house dress, cut and trimmed with a view of making the figure exceedingly stout. (See chapter on "Costumes" in Townsend's "AMATEUR THEATRICALS"— a valuable book, which we mail for 25 cts.) *Act II.*—Outing dress. *Act III.*—Same, change to evening dress.

EFFIE.—*Act I.*—Handsome tea gown. *Act II.*—Outing suit. *Act III.*—Same, change to evening dress.

PROPERTIES.

ACT I.—Newspapers; decanter of cold tea and glass; a dozen packages, large and small, one of which contains a pair of light trousers; several pillows and blankets.

ACT II.—Table cloth, dishes, cups, knives, forks, etc., for luncheon; two bottles of wine, one red, one white; wine glasses; gun to fire; cigars and matches; two baskets, one very large; umbrella.

ACT III.—Cigar and matches; three large pistols.

SYNOPSIS OF EVENTS FOR PROGRAMMES.

ACT I.—Home of the Pictons. Plunker and the press. "Another speculation gone to smash!" A pair of schemers. The coy widow and her admirers. Plunker takes a tumble and Chuggs makes love. Plunker tries his hand. A drink of "nectar." A surprise. "It's vinegar, that's what." Tom and his troubles. Mrs. Billowby is shocked. More vinegar. "What the deuce have I done now?" Tony's glad arrival. Makes matters worse. The broker turns doctor. Some tall medical tales. "So weak his voice fell whenever he spoke." "Cured! Well, rather!" The dashing young widow. Some sage advice. "Always make a man think you know less than he does." Tony and Fanny. Lovers' quarrels. Tony's inspiration. Tom gets a sudden attack. The "doctor's" opinion. "If life should suddenly cease, he would die at once!" Tony's ultimatum. Tom gets sicker. "Shiver now, shiver!" Alarm! Triumph! A joyful dance. Caught in the act. Climax!

ACT II.—Time, the next afternoon. A picnic in the woods. Music and mirth. Chuggs and Plunker in a row. "Two fool dogs quarrelling over a bone." A sudden peace. Tony has a new scheme. A triple elopement. "Tony, you're going it!" Tom's flirtation. "This is t-tough business for me. Wish I'd got a few pointers." Effie's rage. Tony's sympathy. "I could kill them both!" "They might not like it. People are *so* unreasonable." Tony's plan. The plot thickens. Tom in earnest. Trouble begins. "Now, Tony dear, I'm all ready!" General surprise. Mrs. Billowby is also "all ready." More surprise. "He's going to elope with me." "No, he isn't, he's going to elope with *me!*" War in the camp. Effie caps the climax. "I'm all ready!" The "doctor" gets "roasted." "Speak, sir, speak!" Confusion!

ACT III.—Time, evening of same day. Home from the picnic. Tom's opinion. Bombshell No. 1. Effie in a rage. "I want revenge!" "But I haven't got any." Bombshell No. 2. Anastasia's martial tread. More revenge wanted. A feminine fracas. Fanny moralizes. Tom gets a "bracer." Preparing for the fray. The "doctor" gives instructions. A tearful trio. "Where does he lie?" A triple challenge. Ready for gore. The famous three-cornered duel. "I'll plunk Plunker, he can chug Chuggs, and Chuggs can chug me." A halt in the fray. Effie pleads. "There is no law to prevent doctors from killing people." Unconditional surrender. The "doctor" triumphs. No doctor at all— just a plain stockbroker. A final prescription.

4

REMARKS ON THE PLAY.

In presenting this brilliant and successful comedy, we call particular attention to the fact that herein wit and humor are most happily mingled. In most of his comedy work TOWNSEND is more humorous than witty, since the fun arising from comic situations and droll speeches is more palpable than that from incisive wit. But in THE DOCTOR he gives us many witty passages, and these require nice handling. A speech which might be made to convey a double meaning—as in the first scene between *Tom* and *Effie* in Act Third—must be delivered with an air of utter simplicity, thus destroying any hint of *double entente.*

THE DOCTOR is a comic play, lying clearly within the domain of farce, inasmuch as it does not attack any foible or folly of mankind and its mirth does not always follow the lines of strict probability. It has proved, however, to be one of the liveliest, brightest and most laughable plays ever written, and with its short cast—every rôle being strictly first class —it is a prime favorite.

It is printed directly from the author's prompt copy, and from him we have secured the following valuable suggestions regarding each character, which should be carefully studied.

HOPPER. This is the "star" part and should be in the hands of a dashing light comedian. HOPPER is about 25 years of age. He should make up as a blonde, wear a light, curly wig, no beard, and, while sprightly in action, he should carefully avoid over-acting. Deliver his lines with a snap, for the part will bear no dragging, and drive his long "patter" speeches in the first and last acts through with a rush.

TOM is a young fellow of Hopper's age, but is his direct opposite in every way. He is slow in action and slow of speech. His lines must be delivered with an occasional hitch, but be very careful to avoid anything like a stutter. Tom is an easy-going fellow, with very little grit. Still he must not be played like a namby-pamby dude, for that would spoil the part. Make him up without much color, and wear no beard unless it be a light mustache.

CHUGGS is a man of 65. His hair is gray, face pale, and he is either smooth shaven or a long, iron-gray full beard may be worn. He is a type of the smooth, oily, sanctimonious old schemer, who is always on the lookout for number one. Remember, though, that he is not a whining canter, so don't make his speeches drawl nor drag. This part should be played by a tall, slender man if possible.

PLUMPER is a man of 45. He is red-faced, brisk, lively, stout and bumptious. A half-bald red wig and a red chin beard should be worn. Plumper is explosive, loud, noisy and gingery. He is always in a hurry, and the part—being one of broad low comedy—should be exaggerated somewhat.

FANNY is a young widow of 21 and is a type of the lively, dashing young American woman. She should dress rather catchy, and the part must be played with an utter freedom from restraint. Deliver her speeches with a brisk snap,. and carefully avoid posing, for the rôle won't allow it.

MRS. BILLOWBY is a widow of 40—"fat and fair." She should not be played like the conventional mother-in-law, as she is "marriageable," and naturally wishes to create a favorable impression. In drawing this character I made no attempt to give it depth, as it is wholly a surface creation. Mrs. Billowby changes with every breeze, and therefore should be presented in a farcical light throughout.

EFFIE is about 21 ; and as the part may be said to play itself, it calls for no particular description, as the lines and indicated business are sufficient.

TO THE STAGE MANAGER. Whether this play be produced by amateurs without charge, or by professionals under royalty, I wish to caution Stage Managers to look after the climaxes of each act with the utmost care. If there are any delays as the climax approaches, the interest falls and can rarely be regained. This is true of all comedy climaxes, and especially so in plays of this sort when the curtain goes down on a whirlwind of fun. See that the cues are picked up with celerity, and insist that the play shall not go on until all are letter perfect.

THE DOCTOR.

ACT I.

Scene.—*Handsomely furnished room* in fourth grooves, with interior backing in fifth grooves. Curtained arch C. Doors R. 2 E. and L. 2 E. Window L. 3 E. Table and chairs L. front. Tête-à-tête R. front.

Discover PLUNKER *at table reading newspaper.*

Pl. (*reads*). "Wedding bells—Great Divorce Case—An Impressive Funeral." Um! **Love, law and physic!** Anything that escapes the eye **of the great American repo**rter must get up and hustle. Speaking of **hustling,** let's have a look at the market reports. "Lead heavy, **feathers** light, **and** quinine a drug in the market." Exactly. Eh, what's this? "The stock of the Plunker Motor Company took a tremendous tumble on the discovery that the motor would not mote." Another speculation gone to smash! Bungslam the luck! **Who** wants a motor to **mote?** Who wants an invention to **do** anything except float **stock?** Conblast the wobbly gumgasted newspaper! (*Stamps on paper, as* CHUGGS **enters** C.) There! now look me in the face will you, you scandalous libeller of struggling genius!

Chug. Ah! **Mr.** Plunker, you should not abuse the press. Next to attending **a** funeral or strolling through a bright and cheerful graveyard, I enjoy reading the newspapers, especially the dear old jokes—so full of sad and soulful memories.

Pl. Then you—*you* like fun?

Ch. Fun? No, sir. You know there is nothing funny in a comic paper.

Pl. There would be if *you* were in it.

Ch. Eh! Do I look like a funny man?

Pl. Tremendously. You're the most solemn funny-looking cuss I ever saw. You'd make a baboon grin. Ha, ha, ha!

Ch. So I observe.

Pl. Sir! Look here, sir, do you mean to infer——

Ch. Whatever you please, sir—yes, sir.

7

Pl.   Do you know who I am, sir ?

Ch.   Beyond doubt.   You are a done-up old speculator on the lookout for a rich widow, and you won't get her.

Pl.   Why, you old jugger-wugger, I—I——   [*Bus.*

Enter MRS. BILLOWBY, C.

Mrs. B.   Good-afternoon, gentlemen.

Pl. (L.).   My dear madam——   } [*Both bow as she*
Ch. (R.).   My dear Mrs. Billowby——   } *turns up stage.*

Pl.   Get out of my way, you old sag-wap !

Ch.   You—you—you exploded theory !

Mrs. B.   Gentlemen, I want a seat.

Pl.   Of course——   [*Grasps a chair.*

Ch.   Why, certainly.   [*Grasps same chair.   Struggle.*

Mrs. B.   Gentlemen !

[CHUGGS *drops chair*.   PLUNKER *tumbles over*.   CHUGGS *gives another chair to* MRS. B., *who sits.*

Ch.   A triumph of mind over matter.

Mrs. B.   I hope you did not hurt your head, professo ·

Pl. (*dismally*).   My *head* is all right, but—um—my—
          [*Limps off* L.

Ch.   I think that Plunker has joggled his brains.

Mrs. B.   Mr. Chuggs, I am surprised at your hilarity.

Ch.   My hilarity ?   I beg your pardon, my dear Mrs. Billowby, but I have never been hilarious since I became a resident of this wickedly sinful world.

Mrs. B.   And such a sad world, too.   Ah, Mr. Chuggs, you have never known what it is to lose a husband

Ch.   No ; I never lost a husband.

Mrs. B.   Some people fail to appreciate the joys of adversity. There's Mrs. Mayfair : her husband has been dead less than two years, and yet, instead of tribulating as she ought, she flies in the face of Providence and enjoys life.

Ch.   Shocking !   Positively shocking !

Mrs. B.   Isn't it ?   And there's my son-in-law.   Ah, Mr. Chuggs, you have never, *never* known what it is to be a mother-in-law.

Ch.   No, Mrs. Billowby, I have never, *never* been a mother-in-law.

Mrs. B.   Such work as it is.   My daughter is a lamb who would enjoy the sadness and sorrow of this world if it were not for her husband.   But Thomas Picton is a heavy burden for me. Ah, if I only had some strong soul to lean upon.

Ch.   Why resist the dictation of fate ?   Mrs. Billowby— Anastasia—may I call you by that heavenly cognomen ?   Anastasia, I swear——

Mrs. B.   Oh, Mr. Chuggs !

Ch. In a moral way—I swear—— (*Sees* PLUNKER ; *aside.*) Hang that Plunker ! [*Crosses* R.

Enter PLUNKER, **L.**

Mrs. B. Oh, Mr. Plunker !

Pl. (*limps*). Oh, Mrs. Billowby !

Mrs. B. Are you so badly injured ?

Pl. Injured ? I'm a railroad collision and a steamboat explosion all in one.

Mrs. B. I'm so sorry. You need a stimulant. There's some wine in the dining-room. Won't you please run and fetch it, Mr. Chuggs ?

Ch. I'll fly. (*Aside.*) I hope it's the earthquake variety.
[**Exit,** *slowly,* R.

Pl. (*aside*). When I see him I always think of a club.

Mrs. B. And you were injured while endeavoring to serve me ! Oh, Mr. Plunker, I can never forgive myself.

Pl. My dear Mrs. Billowby, to forgive is divine.

Mrs. B. You make such delightful speeches. Do you really think me——

Pl. Divine ? More than that—more than that. Divinity cuts no figure with you.

Mrs. B. Ah, Mr. Plunker !

Pl. Ah, Mrs. Billowby !

Mrs. B. You flatter poor me.

Pl. Impossible. Pierce the blue dome of the high-arched heavens ; dive into the bottomless bottom of the bottomless sea, and yet I could not find words in *which* to say—— (*Sees* CHUGGS.) Oh, blast that old kangaroo !
[*Goes* L. *as* CHUGGS **enters** R. *with decanter and glass.*

Ch. (R.). Here you are ; allow me. [*Fills glass.*

Mrs. B. (C.). Thank you ; allow me.

Pl. (*receives glass from* MRS. B.). My *dear* madam !

Ch. (*holds up decanter ; aside*). It's vinegar !

Pl. A draught from this fair hand is like unto the nectar of the gods ! (*Drinks.*) Ach ! (*Chokes.*) Gr-r- ! Woóch ! Yah ! Gah ! Ugh ! [*Staggers to seat,*

Mrs. B. What's the matter ?

Pl. The gumgasted, ugh, yah, vinegar !

Mrs. B. *and* **Ch.** Vinegar ?

Enter EFFIE, **R.**

Ef. Why, mamma, what *is* the matter ?

Mrs. B. The professor drank some vinegar by mistake——

Ch. (*half aside*). And astonished his stomach as though it had been water !

Enter TOM, C., *with numerous bundles.*

Ef.   Why, Thomas, what a load !

Tom (*stands* C.).   Yes, my dear.

Mrs. B. (*rapidly*).   Where on earth have you been so long ?
Did you get me the white veil and match the Berlin wool ?
Did you secure a copy of Mr. Doleful's last sermon on scandal-
mongers, and *did* you investigate that story about Mrs. High-
flyer and her coachman ?   And you brought my robe, and you
gave that stupid dressmaker a piece of my mind ?

Ef. (*rapidly*).   And you looked up those bargains in damask
—and you got my gloves—and you made arrangements for our
picnic—and you——

Tom (*throws packages on table*).   Yas.   Everything is there.
Help yourselves. (*Aside.*)   Thank heaven Tony Hopper will
be here to-day.   He'll get me out of this mess.

[MRS. B. *and* EFFIE *at table.*

Pl.   And you invested in the Plunker motor stock ?

Tom.   No—d-damn 'f I did !   I draw a line at your motor.

Mrs. B. (*at* C. *with large package*)..   I suppose this is my
robe.   I *do* hope it will fit, for I'm sure—— (*Opens package
displaying pair of light-colored trousers.*)   Ah ! (*Screams
and flings trousers around* PLUNKER'S *neck.*)   Ah !   Support
me. [CHUGGS *catches her.*

Ch.   Heavens !   Support *me !*

[PLUNKER *backs against him.*

Ef.   Give her something—oh, mamma !

Tom.   Yas—g-give her something—oh, mamma !   Here, (*takes
decanter,*) open her m-mouth, somebody. (*Aside.*)   It's closed
for the first time in her life.   Drink, mamma !

[*She swallows, chokes, sputters, and stands erect.* CHUGGS
and PLUNKER *stagger back, glare and* exeunt R. *and* L.

Mrs. B.   You w-wretch !

[*Crosses and sits.* EFFIE *joins her.*

Tom (*blankly*).   What in b-blazes have I done now ? (*Places
decanter on table.*)   Hello ! (*Looks through window.*)   By
J-Jove, he's arrived !

Ef.   Who ?

Tom.   Tony Hopper.

Ef.   Tony Hopper ?   Who is he ?

Tom.   The best fellow that ever lived, and a man every inch
of him.

Dil. (*off* C.).   Tom, old boy !

Tom (*at* C.).   This way !

[**Exit** C., *re-entering immediately with* DILLINGTON
HOPPER.

Dil.   Tom !

Tom.   Let's have a look at you.   Jove !   N-natural as ever.

Dil. The same old coon, my boy.

Tom. Not married?

Dil. No, thank heaven!

Mrs. B. Oh!

Dil. Eh?

Tom. Hush—I am! Allow me. Mrs. Billowby, Effie, my dear, let me present my oldest and best friend, Dillington Hopper, of New York.

Dil. Ladies, your devoted. Mrs. Picton, you are a living witness of Tom's rare taste and better luck. But he always was a devil of a fellow among the ladies.

Ef. and Mrs. B. Oh!

Dil. Eh?

Tom (*aside*). Confound him!

Dil. Aren't you well, Mrs. Billowby?

Mrs. B. I'm nearly dead.

Ef. Tom gave dear mamma something that disagreed with her.

Tom (*aside*). And dear mamma *always* disagrees with *me*.

Dil. (*to* MRS. B.). My dear madam, you should not mind a little thing like that. When you know Tom as well as I do, you will not be surprised at anything he does. These quiet fellows are always the worst reprobates. (*To* TOM.) I know you of old, you sinner!

Mrs. B. (*horrified*). What do I hear?

Ef. My husband a sinner?

Tom (*to* DIL.). For heaven's sake let up.

Dil. It's all right, ladies—fact, I assure you. No doubt Tom has sown his wild oats before this.

Mrs. B. I watch Mr. Picton's morals, sir, as closely as I do my own.

Dil. Then I am sure that with such a guiding hand he never strays. I am glad that he has reformed, but it is nothing short of a miracle. Was he really so dreadfully dreadful?

Ef. Was he really so dreadfully dreadful?

Mrs. B. Effie!

Dil. Dreadful? He was simply—I say, Tom, do you remember——

Tom. Yas—never mind.

Ef. Go on, Mr. Hopper!

Dil. —that night at the masquerade ball when you danced the——

Tom. I'll m-murder you!

Ef. Go on, Mr. Hopper, go on!

Dil. When you danced the what-you-may-call-it?

Ef. Oh!

Mrs. B. My poor, precious lamb, I greatly fear that you have been deceived in Mr. Thomas Picton.

Ef. To think that my husband ever danced the what—(*sobs*) what—what-you-may-call-it !

Mrs. B. I shall demand a full explanation, Mr. Thomas Picton, regarding that what-you-may-call-it ! Come, my poor, dear, injured innocence !   [*They* exeunt R.

Dil. It strikes me that I've put my foot in it.

Tom (*seated*). You've played the very d-devil with me.

Dil. My dear fellow, if I've got you into a scrape I must pull you out somehow. Let me diagnose your case. (Enter MRS. B., R.) Place yourself in my hands, make me your doctor, and I will guarantee to cure anything from a fit of the blues to a bad conscience.

Mrs. B. A doctor? Excuse me, Mr. Hopper, but did I understand that you're a doctor ?

Dil. Madam, I——

Tom (*to him*). S-say yas.

Dil. Certainly, madam.

Tom (*aside*). Now I've g-got him !

Mrs. B. I am overjoyed to hear it, for I am so dreadfully delicate. Then I may depend on your services ?

Dil. Certainly you may. (*Aside.*) Here's a go !

Tom (*aside*). Now I *have* g-got him !

Mrs. B. I must consult you regarding myself—describe my symptoms, you know.

Dil. (*aside*). O Lord ! She's going to describe her symptoms !

Mrs. B. And my daughter isn't very well. I want you to find out what is the matter with her.

Dil. (*cheerfully*). All right.

Tom (*aside*). I'll be d-damned if he does !

Mrs. B. And is my son-in-law threatened with disease ?

Dil. Threatened ? My dear Mrs. Billowby, I fear that he is doomed to die if he lives long enough, and possibly if he doesn't. I was about looking him over as you came in. Now, my poor friend, let me see your tongue.

Tom. Oh, come now, I s-say——

Dil. No words ! Come ! (TOM *shows tongue.*) More ! Still more ! More yet ! All of it ! (*Feels pulse.*) Ah—too bad, too bad, *too* bad !

Mrs. B. What is it, doctor ?

Dil. Just as I feared, just as I feared. The specific genu-flections of the lymphatic dactyls indicate a marked inflexibility of the dia-pho-ret-ico-pan-tha-ca-thol-icon ! Do you follow me ?

Mrs. B. Mercy on us !

Tom. Is it catching ?

Dil. Moreover there is a predisposition towards an acute inflammation of the *thalami nevorum opticorum!* This, if not checked, will eventually lead to consumption, rheumatism, fits, intemperance, insanity, corns, bunions and poor health! Do you follow me?

Mrs. B. Oh, doctor! Is there danger?

Dil. Danger, my dear Mrs. Billowby? Danger? Why, my dear madam, if life should cease he would die at once!

Mrs. B. If life should suddenly cease he would die at once! Oh, doctor, what *is* to be done?

Dil. I think we better soak his head, put mustard plasters on his feet and send for the undertaker.

Tom. You had? Now I can't see the joke in that.

Dil. After all, the old treatment may be best.

Mrs. B. The old treatment?

Tom (*aside*). What's c-coming now?

Dil. There are people so constituted that excitement is necessary to preserve their health. My poor friend is one of these unfortunates. Therefore when he drank champagne and danced the what-you-may-call-it——

Mrs. B. In a moral way?

Dil. Why, certainly—he was then following my directions.

Tom. You're a b-brick!

Mrs. B. How much we are indebted to you, doctor, and how modestly you speak of it.

Dil. My dear madam, you overpower me. I certainly *am* very modest, though I strive to conceal the fact!

Tom (*aside*). O Jupiter!

Dil. If you will excuse us for a short time I will continue my examination, as I wish to learn whether I must prescribe the old round of excitement—in a moral way.

Mrs. B. (*goes* L.). Very well. (*Aside.*) Isn't he delightful! And a doctor, too! Ah me! I'm sure that my heart is affected. [Exit L.

Dil. Now, my boy, you wrote that you're in trouble. What's the matter?

Tom. My mother-in-law, and I've g-got her bad. Tony, old man, if ever you have the choice between marrying a girl with a m-mother and jumping off the dock, don't hesitate— j-jump.

Dil. Poor devil! Why not make a tremendous kick?

Tom. It's all right to t-talk, but how's a fellow to kick with both l-legs tied down?

Dil. You have got me into trouble very likely by making me a doctor. At the same time, if I can help you I will.

Tom. You can, and it's dead easy. Marry m-mamma.

Dil. Marry Beelzebub!

Tom. We won't argue that. She's rich, good-looking, on

the right side of forty, warranted sound, and g-guaranteed not to shy.

Dil. But, my dear fellow——

Tom. Oh, she'll have you.

Dil. But I don't want her.

Tom. Very well—then t-take her out and lose her. Is it a go?

Dil. I should say not. It's an utter impossibility. I'll be your friend forever, but hang me if I'll be your father.

Tom. Then I may as well b-blow out my brains.

Dil. Don't. It might kill you.

Tom. Yas—I never thought of that.

Dil. Look here, Tom. You have made me a doctor in spite of myself. Very good. Now the *best* thing is to prescribe for you in earnest.

Tom. Yes—but I can't see the joke in that.

Dil. It's no joke. You may live through it ; if not, I'll do what I can to make your last hours easy. And if you die, you will certainly get rid of your mother-in-law.   [*They go* R.

Tom. Yas—that's one comfort.

Dil. All right. Then we'll rehearse our little drama " The Broker Turned Doctor, or the Son-in-Law's Revenge ! "

[*Exeunt* R.

Hopper ready R.

Enter MRS. BILLOWBY, L.

Mrs. B. Dear me, I wish he would finish with Tom, for I want to see about—— (*Looks through window.*) Good gracious ! If there isn't that human cyclone, Fanny Mayfair, rushing up the steps in her usual whirlwind manner. It's positively outrageous the way she races through life. I can't endure her.

Enter FANNY MAYFAIR, C.

Fan. Anastasia !

Mrs. B. Fanny ! (*Embrace.*) I'm *so* glad to see you.

Fan. I thought I'd surprise you, my dear, so I had my groom saddle the Devil——

Mrs. B. Fanny!

Fan. That's my horse—Dare Devil ; I usually drop the prefix. I wish you would have your men cautioned to look out for him. He's playful with his heels. Where's Tom?

Mrs. B. Closeted with his physician—a brilliant man.

Fan. Is Tom sick ?

Mrs. B. Very likely. We don't know for certain. The doctor is trying to find out.

Fan. Indeed ? I should like to meet this brilliant doctor. (*Aside.*) I'll bet he's a regular quack.

Mrs. B. Here he comes now.   [FANNY *turns* L.

Enter HOPPER, R.

Mrs. B. Oh, doctor, how is he ?

Dil. 'Sh ! **Keep** quiet. I'll **tell you** shortly.

Mrs. B. Very well. Excuse **me**, doctor, but here **is a lady** who wishes **to know you.**

Fan. (*aside*). **Oh,** the spiteful **thing !**

Dil. I shall be delighted.

Mrs. B. Mrs. Mayfair—Dr. Dillington Hopper.

Dil. (*aside*). Fanny ! Now **for an** earthquake !

Fan. (*aside*). Tom ! Well, I **never !**

Mrs. B. Fanny dear, will you kindly entertain **the doctor** while I go look for Effie ?

Fan. (L.). Don't be long.

Mrs. B. I will not. (*Up* C.) **Catch** me leaving **that** innocent young **man** very long with her. [**Exit** C.

Dil. (R.). **This** is an odd meeting, Mrs. Fanny Mayfair.

Fan. Very odd indeed, *Doctor* Dillington Hopper ! Ha, ha, ha ! What a **delicious** fraud **you are** !

Dil. I dare say.

Fan. Then you admit——

Dil. That I am **playing the doctor ? Certainly.** I assumed the rôle to help Tom.

Fan. Is Tom **in** trouble?

Dil. Yes—he's married.

Fan. Happy **man !**

Dil. Well—he'll **serve as** an awful warning. See **what** *I* might **have been** if you had not so shamefully ill-used me.

Fan. I ? **Well,** if that isn't impudence !

Dil. Oh, deny it, deny it, of course.

Fan. Certainly I do. It was *you*, **sir,** who ill-used *me*.

Dil. What charming assurance !

Fan. Were you not insanely jealous ?

Dil. Didn't you flirt with every fool you met ?

Fan. I **never** flirted **with** you.

Dil. Good reason **why :** I wouldn't let a coq**uette make a** blooming **idiot** of me.

Fan. No, for nature kindly spared the coquette that trouble.

Dil. Married life has sharpened you tongue, **Mrs.** Fanny Mayfair.

Fan. And single **life** your temper, *Doctor* Dillington Hopper. But there : **we** quarrelled when we last **met.** Now let us patch **up a** truce. Come—be pleasant, and I **will** promise to flirt **with** nobody **else** forever **so** long—a whole **hour** at least.

Dil. You have not changed a particle. You are the same heartless, heedless, **beautiful,** lovable mystery as **ever.**

Fan. And **you** are the same quick-tempered, good-hearted, handsome, dashing man about town that you always were. Am I not right.

Dil. A lovely woman is always right.

Fan. Good—then we're friends again ?.

Dil. Friends ? My dear Fanny, I'll not stop at friendship, for——

Fan. Ah ! Remember, I'm the same "heedless, heartless "——

Dil. I never meant a word of it.

Fan. Beautiful, lovable——

Dil. I mean—I meant—I—oh, hang it all !

Fan. We shall see. But how about Tom ?

Dil. Poor devil. You see he has a mother-in-law and several other birds of prey fastened to him. By a lucky inspiration I'm made a doctor. I make him sick, scare away the birds, and Tom is himself again. Love, joy, peace, slow fire, red curtain, tumti tumti, bing, bang, bung, like Wagner's music—better than it sounds.

Fan. Bravo !

Dil. Good scheme, eh ?

Fan. Splendid ! Oh, what a lark ! Count me in, I'll be your partner.

Dil. For life ?

Fan. Hush—here comes Effie.

Dil. Then I'll look after Tom. Remember now, you must help me out.

Fan. All right.   [DIL. exit R.

Enter EFFIE, C.

Fan. My dear Effie.   [*Embrace.*

Ef. What an age since we met !   [*They sit.*

Fan. And so you are married. How does it seem ?

Ef. Well—it's—er—nice and all that, and Tom is just splendid —but—you see——

Fan. I see. Every couple is not a pair.

Ef. It isn't that. We get along nicely—we agree in everything, for dear Tom always agrees with me. But I am afraid that he considers dear mamma something of a—a——

Fan. Nuisance ?

Ef. Well——

Fan. My love, did Tom marry you or your mother ?

Ef. The idea ! But you see, Fanny dear, Tom is not literary, and mamma is helping me cultivate him.

Fan. Don't you do it.

Ef. Why not ?

Fan. My dear Effie, I have been a woman for several years.

During that time I have made **a very** careful study of that interesting animal we call man.

Ef. Yes—well?

Fan. The average man is vainer than a peacock. If a woman is bright and pretty **he** admires her, provided she knows less, or pretends to know less, than himself. But the moment that she assumes **an air** of superior wisdom **his** vanity **is touched and** he bolts. **By the way,** what visitors have you?

Ef. Dr. Hopper for one—and Mr. Chuggs, a philanthropist.

Fan. Yes—he gives **away** other people's money.

Ef. Prof. Plunker, the inventor, is here also.

Fan. And the Plunker still flourishes? **I thought he was** dead.

Ef. Oh, no. He resides in Philadelphia.

Fan. And **pray** what **is the difference**?

Ch. (*outside*). **It's ridi**culous, **sir, ridi**culous.

Pl. (*outside*). **Science,** sir, is never ridiculous.

Ef. Here they come, and quarrelling as usual.

Enter CHUGGS *and* PLUNKER, C.

Ch. **I tell you it's** an impossible humbug, sir!

Pl. **It's** no such thing, sir.

Ef. **Oh,** dear! Fanny, **allow me.** Mr. Chuggs, Prof. Plunker—Mrs. Mayfair.   [*All bow very low.*

Ch. (R.). Most happy to meet you, Mrs. Mayfair.

Pl. (L.). Delighted beyond measure, Mrs. Mayfair.

Ch. Happiest moment of my——

Pl. **I assure** you that——

>   [*Together. Approach, bowing, collide, glare,*
>   *and go up* R. *and* L.

Fan. (C.). It's a dead heat! All bets are off!

Ef. Ah, you rogue! Two fresh victims.

Fan. Stuff! Do you call *those* fresh?   [*They* **go up** C.

Enter MRS. BILLOWBY, C.

Mrs. B. Oh dear! oh dear!   [*Sobs.*

Ef. What **is the matter,** mamma?

Mrs. B. It's Tom and the—the—cat!

Fan. Tom and the cat?

Ch. She means the Thomas **cat.**

Pl. Maybe **he** saw **a** mouse.

Fan. *and* **Ef.** A mouse? Oh-h!   [*They get on chairs.*

Mrs. B. No—there was no m-m-mouse.

Fan. Then what's all this fuss about?   [*Comes down* C.

Mrs. B. **He** was on the table——

Fan. Who, Tom?

Mrs. B. No, the cat. **And** he ate **up** all the d-devil——

2

Pl.   The devil ?

Mrs. B.   *No*, sir !   The devilled crabs.   And **he's** got the consumption, too !

Fan.   Who ?—the cat ?

Mrs. B.   *No*—Tom.   The doctor says he'll surely die.   And when he saw me coming he growled and humped up his back, and——

Omnes.   *Who—Tom ?*

Mrs. B. (*crossly*).   *No*—the cat.

Pl. (*aside*).   Oh, rats !

Enter HOPPER *and* TOM, c.

Dil. (*supporting* TOM).   **Easy,** my poor friend, easy now.

Ef.   Oh, doctor !   [DIL. *helps* TOM *to seat.*

Dil.   'Sh !   Keep quiet—don't excite him.

Ef.   Is he——

Dil.   He is.   It's a desperate case.   **Keep** quiet.

Ch.   But what ails him ?

Dil.   A more or less complicated variety of disorders.   I fear that he is a mere shell **as it were,** full of deadly material and liable to explode at any **time.**   His drooping figure—(*To* TOM.) Droop, **droop** !—his drooping figure indicates a sudden failing of the vital powers.   His sad looks—(*To* TOM.)   Look sad, look sad —his sad looks show that at best he fears the worst.   Besides that, his consumptive cough—*cough,* confound you, cough ! (TOM *coughs.*)   Don't be alarmed, don't be alarmed.   (*To* TOM.) Keep it up, **keep** it up !

Ef.   Oh, doctor, do you—*is* there any danger ?

Dil.   No doubt of it, especially if it runs into small-pox or yellow fever.

Ch. *and* **Pl.**   Small-pox ?   [*They bolt for* C. D.

Dil.   Hold on now, hold on.   It hasn't gone that far—yet.

Mrs. B.   Then you can save him ?

Dil.   Save him, my dear madam ?   Why, certainly.   Consumption is my hobby, and I may say without boasting that I never lost a case.

Tom (*aside*).   I'll swear to that.

Ch. (*aside*).   What gorgeous liars these doctors are !

Ef.   But this is an unusual case, is it not ?

Dil.   Very unusual.   I never saw one like it before.

Tom (*aside*).   I'll swear to *that.*

Dil.   Still I have seen others equally bad.   I recall one of more than forty years' standing.   He had taken more than a hundred varieties of sure cure for consumption, and therefore was nearly dead.   He was very weak—couldn't hold his breath without dropping it, and his voice fell whenever he spoke. Lungs all gone, too—breathed through his gills like a fish.

Foot tub and tea kettle ready R.

Mrs. B. And you cured him ?

Dil. Cured him ? I think yes. So thoroughly that nobody knew him. Had to get out a writ of *habeas corpus* to prove who he was.

Pl. (*aside*). Oh, if I could only lie like that !

Dil. Tom will recover if my orders are strictly obeyed.

Ef. They shall be.

Dil. But if opposition arises——

Mrs. B. I'll sit down on any opposition.

Tom (*aside*). I p-pity the opposition !

Dil. Tom needs absolute quiet. Nobody can remain here except his wife, the servants and myself.

Ef. Not even mamma ?

Dil. Not even mamma.

Mrs. B. But really, doctor, *I* must remain.

Ch. Yes, doctor, *we* must remain.

Tom. O Lord—the d-devil—I say——

Dil. Hush ! Tom has another attack. It's a chill. He's all in a shiver. (*To* TOM.) Shiver now, shiver !

Tom. I c-can't. It's too blamed hot.

Fan. Run—everybody run—hurry ! Get hot water—liquor —flannel—something, anything, everything !

Dil. Yes, yes ! Hurry ! (*To* TOM.) Shiver, confound you ! —Hurry up ! It's a case of life and death ! (*To* TOM.) Keep it up, keep it up !

> [*General movement.* MRS. B. *and* EFFIE *run off* R. CHUGGS *and* PLUNKER *start* L., *tumble over each other, rise, glare, shake their fists and* exeunt L.

Tom. I s-say—do you mean to roast me ?

Fan. No, it's only a ruse.

Dil. We've won the day !

Fan. Hurrah for us !

Tom. I believe I'm c-cured !

> [*Jumps up ; all join in dance. When at its height*

Enter OMNES, R. *and* L., *carrying pillows, blankets, etc.*

Mrs. B. Ah ! [*Screams and drops bundle.*

Ch. Sold !

Pl. Another speculation busted !

Mrs. B. Support me ! [*Staggers.*

Fan. Everybody faint !

> [*Brisk movement.* FANNY *and* EFFIE *fall into* HOPPER'S *arms. He tosses* EFFIE *to* TOM. MRS. BILLOWBY *falls into* CHUGGS' *arms, who staggers against* PLUNKER, *knocking him down.* CHUGGS *falls into chair with* MRS. B., *who springs up indignantly.*

CURTAIN.

ACT II.

Scene.—*Woodland. Full **stage**. Sunlight effects. Wings **and** sinks trees and foliage. Set rocks up* L. *Stump of tree* R. *Mossy **bank*** L. *Cloth **spread*** C., *with remnant of luncheon.*

Discover MRS. BILLOWBY *seated* C., *eating ;* CHUGGS *and* PLUNKER *beside her, drinking **wine** ;* MRS. MAYFAIR *and* EFFIE **on** *bank.* TOM *on stump. Introduce **song** and chorus.*

Ch. Now I call this enjoying life. Here we are in the breezy woods, far from the maddening crowd, taking pleasure in moderation.   [*Drinks.*

Mrs. B. Mr. Chuggs, a toast, a toast !

All. Hear, hear !

Ch. (*raising glass*). A warm friend and a jolly one ; a true wife and a pretty one ; a good drink (*drinks*) and another one.
                                              [*Drinks.*

All. Bravo !   [CHUGGS *and* PLUNKER *stroll up*

Ef. Tom, mamma wants you.

Tom. Yes, my dear. (*Aside.*) It's no use. Tony's scheme wasn't worth a c-continental. I've got that nightmare worse than ever.   [*Crosses to* MRS. B.

Mrs. B. Where is the doctor ?

                          [MRS. MAYFAIR *strolls up* L.

Tom. He stopped for a little shooting down by the lake.

Mrs. B. (*hands to ears*). Shooting ! Oh !

Tom. You're all right. (*Aside.*) He isn't h-hunting for cats !

Fan. What does he expect to shoot ?

Pl. A ram-slam mosquito maybe. They're big as geese out here.

Tom. Or a spider. There's a big one on you.

Mrs. B. (*rising*). Ouch ! Wooch ! Take it off ! Kill it !

Tom. It's all right. You've scared it to death.
                                          [*Joins* EFFIE.

Fan. (*seated on stump*). I'm choking with thirst

Mrs. B. So am I.

Pl. (*grabs bottle from basket*). Champagne, Mrs Mayfair ?

Ch. (*same business*). Claret, Mrs. Billowby ?

Fan. I want claret.

Pl. Certainly, my *dear* madam !

                          [*Takes bottle from* CHUGGS.

Ch. Well, that's cool !   [PLUNKER *fills* FANNY'S *glass.*

Tom. And *he* looks h-hot !

Pl. Of course it's cool. Do you suppose I would **give** a lady warm claret?

Ch. You—you speculative old humbug!

Pl. (*furiously*). You—you—you—wretched old gy-gy——

Tom. He's calling you a g-guy!

Pl. Gyasticus! [*They go up, quarrelling.*

Ef. Oh, Tom, don't let them fight.

Tom. No danger. One's afraid, and the other d-dassent.

Mrs. B. Well, must I perish from th rst?
[*Holds up glass.* CHUGGS *and* PLUNKER *both pour wine into it.*

Tom. Hello! Mamma's taking it mixed!

Ch. (*fills another glass for* MRS. B.). I'll be a Nemesis to old Plunker!

Pl. (*aside*). I'll certainly destroy that old mummy!
[*They go up.*

Mrs. B. Tom!

Tom. Yas?

Mrs. B. What are those giddy men about?

Fan. About three sheets in the wind.

Tom. They're a couple of f-fool dogs, fighting over a bone.

Mrs. B. Thomas Picton, I'm no bone!

Pl. I'll give you a push in the face, sir.

Ch. You're—'ic—liar, sir. I demand satisfaction due gentle-man, sir.

Pl. (*flourishing bottle*). Come—'ic—come 'n' get it.

Ch. (*bottle in each hand*). Yesser—'ic—yesser!
[*They exeunt L. U. E.*

Mrs. B. Thomas Picton, run after those men. Stop them.

Tom. Yas. [*Strolls up L.*

Mrs. B. Do hurry. They'll both kill each other!

Tom. No such good luck as that.
[*Exit slowly L. U. E., followed by MRS. B.*

Ef. Fanny dear!

Fan. (*down C.*). What is it?

Ef. Do you really think Tom is sick?

Fan. Desperately.

Ef. He seemed lively enough yesterday.

Fan. Temporary excitement, my dear. He was overjoyed at the prospect of being alone with you.

Enter TOM, L. U. E.

Ef. Oh, Tom, are they fighting?

Tom. Not n-now.

Fan. What then?

Tom. Running a f-footrace.

Ef. With whom?

Tom. With an infuriated gentleman cow. (MRS. B. *screams.*) There. Mamma has sounded **an** alarm !

[MRS. BILLOWBY *runs on* L. U. E.

Mrs. B. **Save** them, Thomas, save them ! (CHUGGS *and* PLUNKER *yell off* L. U. E.) Oh ! (*Shot fired. All go up.*) Somebody's killed ! I—I know I shall **faint.**

Tom. Wait till Chuggs gets **here.**

Fan. Here **comes** a part of **him.**

Enter CHUGGS *and* PLUNKER, L. U. E. *to* C., *supporting each other, gasping for breath, clothing torn, no hats.*

Tom. They look like a couple of baseball umpires.

Ef. Are you hurt ?

[*They groan. Sit on stump, back to back.*

Mrs. B. Are you killed ?   [*Groans.*

Pl. I was taking care of Chuggs.

Ch. And I was defending Plunker.

Tom. Yas—and your legs were t-taking care of you both.

Enter HOPPER *in hunting costume, with gun, etc.*, L. U. E.

Ef. Oh, **doctor,** you **shot** the cow ?

Dil. Yes, I shot the cow—and the cow was a bull ; however, that's immaterial.

Ch. (*dismally*). I want my hat.

Pl. So do I.

Dil. Go and get them—the **cow** won't kick.

Mrs. B. We will go with you, won't we, Fanny ?

Fan. To be sure. Come, professor. [*They* exeunt L. U. E.

Mrs. B. Now, Mr. Chuggs.   [*Helps him to rise.*

Ch. **What** an angel you are, my dear Mrs. Billowby !

Mrs. B. (*going up* L.). Then there's a pair of us, Mr. Chuggs.

[**Exit** L. U. E.

Tom. Moses !

Ef. I **want** to go fishing. Come, Tom, I **want** you to bait my hook.

Tom. What's the use ? There's nothing but **bull-**heads in the lake.

Ef. Yes ! Then you keep **away** from **the wa**ter.   [Exit R,

Tom. Well, I—I like that !   [Exit R.

Dil. Things are getting decidedly warm here. (*Lights cigar.*) The old lady insists on describing her ailments with a minuteness that is simply awful. What a circus there will be if she discovers that I'm no doctor. I ought to jump out before things tumble, yet I hate to leave Tom in a slump. What the devil **can** I do ? Let—me—see. Eh ? Egad, I have it, I have it ! I'll get Tom to flirting with Fanny ; that will arouse Effie's jealousy. **Then** I will make **love** to Effie—in a moral **way—**

which will put **Tom on** his mettle ; **and then,** hang it, I'll make love to the old **lady—in** a *strictly* moral way—which will bring old Chuggs to **the** point. (**Enter** TOM, R.) Tom, come here. You love your mother-in-law ?

Tom. As the devil loves holy water.

Dil. Then **to get rid** of her——

Tom. Yas——

Dil. Make **love to Fanny.**

Tom. What ? Make love to **Fanny ?**

Dil. Platonic **love.** Effie **weeps,** old lady raves, I console her, get old Chuggs jealous, he roars, raves, marries the old lady, they clear out, leave you alone, all serene, everybody happy. Catch the idea ?

Tom (L.). **Yas.** Make **love to** Fanny——

Dil. (R.). Effie weeps——

Tom. Mamma wails——

Dil. That's the idea. (TOM **exit L. I E.**) Now **for the fire-works.** (*Quickly.*) Fizz, boom—ah ! [**Exit** R. I E.

Enter MRS. BILLOWBY, CHUGGS and PLUNKER, L. U.E.

Hopper ready R.U.E, Fanny ready L.2.E

Mrs. B. Your invention is wonderful—isn't it, Mr. Chuggs ?

Ch. Ah, yes—as wonderful as perpetual motion, or catching a whale in a tub—and just as possible.

Pl. What do you know of science, sir ?

Ch. The same as you, sir.

Pl. And that is——

Ch. Nothing. (*Aside.*) Kee ! Had him **there !**

Mrs. B. It's so nice to be an inventor. Why don't you get up something, Mr. Chuggs ?

Ch. **I am** getting up something. I'm organizing a company,

Pl. For what purpose ?

Ch. To import green cheese from the moon !

Mrs. B. This doesn't **seem** like a **real** picnic.

Ch. Why not ?

Mrs. B. Because it hasn't rained to-day.

Pl. (*aside*). Old **Chuggs** got pretty well soaked anyhow !

Ch. **You are** right, **my dear** madam. I remember that when I was a little **boy**——

Pl. Oh, **come now—don't** give **us** any more antediluvian history. I've heard **all about** the deluge.

Mrs. B. Here, help me pack **up. We** must return soon. (*Business of filling baskets, one of which is very large.*) There, Mr. Chuggs, **you** take this. (*Gives **smaller** basket.*) And you this, (*gives* PLUNKER *the larger basket*) **and** this. (*Throws table cloth over his head.*) There, that's all. Now come on, and don't you dare lose anything.

Ch. My *dear* Mrs. Billowby. [***Offers** arm, which she takes.*

Pl. *My* dear Mrs. Billowby. [*Offers arm.*
Mrs. B. Oh bother! [*Takes his arm also.* Exeunt L. U. E.

Enter HOPPER, R. U. E., *and* FANNY, L. 2 E.

Dil. Fanny !
Fan. Tony !
Dil. (*brings her down*, C.). I've got a scheme !
Fan. Yes ?
Dil. Mum's the word.
Fan. Mum it is.
Dil. H-s-h !
Fan. H-s-h !
Dil. Let's elope.
Fan. Elope ?
Dil. And get married.
Fan. What for ?
Dil. What for ? Why do any people get married ?
Fan. Oh, for various reasons. Men marry for love, and all that.
Dil. And women ?
Fan. Because they know so little about it.
Dil. But a widow should know something about it.
Fan. Ah, that's quite different. A widow, poor thing, learns by bitter experience that the sea of matrimony is very rough sailing.
Dil. Yes, there are some *squalls* now and then.
Fan. When a girl falls in love, she thinks the idol of her heart is simply perfection. She makes him a king in fact, and holds him beyond all price.
Dil. And there she differs from us. No man would set any value on *one* king, though he might bet his last red cent on four of them.
Fan. Now I know what matrimony is like. I've been there.
Dil. Only once, and then you married a man so old that you really adopted a father.
Fan. If I thought you were in earnest——
Dil. In earnest ? My dear Fanny ! In earnest ? Doubt that the stars are fire, doubt that the sun doth move——
Fan. There ! Now stop ! I can stand anything but poetry.
Dil. Then in all seriousness, my darling, I love you as a miser loves gold, as a soldier loves glory, an actor applause and a girl ice-cream.
Fan. I suppose I must believe you.
Dil. Then it's a bargain ?
Fan. Well—yes.
Dil. Signed and delivered. (*Kisses her.*) And now I've

Fan. (*breaking away*). What—another woman?

Dil. Oh no, my dear. H-s-h! I want you to flirt with Tom.

Fan. Excuse *me*.

Dil. And why?

Fan. Because he knows nothing of the art.

Dil. Never mind that.

Fan. But I don't see the point.

Dil. It's plain as a pikestaff. Tom's wife and her mother have his nose on the grindstone. A mild flirtation will arouse his bump of self-esteem. He will assert himself, break loose from their apron strings, bounce the old lady, have a row with his wife, kiss, make up, everything lovely—see? Do you follow me?

Fan. Without a break.

Dil. Here comes the victim. I'll vanish. (*Goes* R.) Now remember, lead trumps and we're bound to win. [**Exit R. U. E.**

Enter TOM, L. U. E. **FANNY** *sits on stump.*

Tom. There she is. I wish **Tony** had given me some p-pointers.

Fan. Why, Tom—Mr. Picton—how you startled me. I was just thinking of you—that is—I—I—you know.

Tom. Yas.

Fan. (*sighs*). Ah!

Tom. What's the m-matter? Aren't you well?

Fan. Why do you ask?

Tom. I don't know. I—I never groan like that unless I have the colic.

Fan. I am quite, quite well, but *very* unhappy.

Tom. Let me console you. Beauty in distress always arouses my p-pity.

Fan. You are so kind—so thoughtful. [*They cross to bank.*

Tom (*seated*). D-don't mention it.

Fan. Ah, me!

Tom. Me too. (*Aside.*) I never made love like this before.

Fan. My dear, dear Tom, have you, too, a hidden grief?

Tom. No—you c-can't hide her.

Fan. Hide whom?

Tom. My mother-in-law. She's my grief.

Fan. How sad you look. It must be a weighty sorrow.

Tom. Yas. She *is* rather heavy.

Fan. And to think what might have been—for I am an orphan.

Tom. Eh? Oh, yas.

Fan. Tom——

Tom. Yas, my dear? [*Arm around her.*

Fan. Tom, what are you doing? Reflect.

Tom. I am. ' I always reflect this way.

Fan. But, Tom dear, it is very, very wrong for you to do this. (*Head on his shoulder.*) You are married, you know.

Tom. Yas. It's wrong for me, but it's all right for you.

Fan. But if Mrs. Billowby should see you——

Tom (*jumping up*). The d-deuce !

Fan. (*indignantly*). Mr. Picton, the next time you intend to have a spasm, I wish you would let me know.

Tom. My dear Fanny, it's all right. I know I'm something of a m-muff, but what the dickens could you expect of a fellow in my place ? And you see when a fellow has found out that he knows what he didn't know before, and makes up his mind that perhaps he *ought* to, the chances are that maybe he *will* some time or another, d-don't you know, unless he c-changes his opinion one *way* or another, so that it will be different more or less from what it had been before he made up his mind differently from the way he—er—— (*Aside.*) Blast it !—Don't you see ?

Fan. Have you any idea of what you are talking about ?

Tom. No—not in particular, except that I—er—love you, Fanny, ever so much—oh yes, I do—so if you're willing we'll astonish the natives, arouse the c-country, alarm the world, and upset the universe by r-running away with each other ! (*Aside.*) M-Moses ! What a mess !

Fan. Tom, dear Tom, your passionate eloquence is so convincing to a poor, weak woman ! I can resist no more ! I *will* run away with you ! [*Throws herself in his arms.*

Tom (*aside*). I *have* made a m-mess of it.

Fan. In a moral way.

Tom (*relieved*). Oh, that's something different. (*They go* L.) Certainly, we can elope in a m-moral way. [**Exeunt** L.

Enter EFFIE *and* HOPPER, R. U. E.

Ef. Did you see that ?

Dil. I did, I did !

Ef. Oh, what an outrage !

Dil. It is, it is.

Ef. Men are all such wretches !

Dil. They are, they are !

Ef. And women are all such fools !

Dil. They are, they are !

Ef. I'll never speak to him again ! I'll tear her eyes out ! I'll commit suicide ! I'll go home to my mother ! I'll get a divorce ! I'll—oh-h !

Dil. My dear Effie, don't get excited. You may have a fit.

Ef. I could kill them both.

Dil. Very likely, but don't. **They** might object. **People** are *so* unreasonable. **Now** I've an idea.

Ef. Well ?

Dil. My plan is free from blood and thunder and coffins and dungeons and other unpleasant things.

Ef. Well, well ?

Dil. In brief, give Tom a dose of his own medicine.

Ef. What !

Dil. Fact. *Similia similibus* **curantur.** Sauce for the gander, sauce for the goose. For instance, run away with me.

Ef. Doctor Hopper !

Dil. It's all right. We'll have an elopement—platonic you know—entirely platonic—but Tom will be none the wiser.

Ef. Splendid ! I'll tell mamma !

Dil. H-sh-h ! Not for the world. Now run over to the farmhouse yonder and write Tom a note. Work in "perfidious wretch," "false vows" and all that sort of thing. Tell him that he has broken your heart—smashed it into pieces—ten thousand or so—never mind the exact number—and wind up by saying that you have found a sympathetic heart which beats in unison with yours—that you have flown away with your affinity—weary head, nest, breast, rest, and so on.

Ef. All right ! Oh-h! What a revenge I'll have !

[Exit L. 1 E.

Dil. The plot is thickening. Effie is charming, lovely, delightful. I *could* run away with her in earnest if it were not for the mother-in-law. And yet, I suppose that mothers-in-law are somewhat necessary ; for, if there were no mothers, I suppose there would be very few daughters.

Enter MRS. BILLOWBY, L. 1 E.

Mrs. B. Such carelessness ! Such stupid, stupid carelessness !

Dil. (*aside*). Hello ! Here's a rod in pickle for somebody.

Mrs. B. Oh, doctor, what do you think !

Dil. My dear madam, when the thermometer gets above ninety-five in the shade I never think.

Mrs. B. That is all right—but we're left.

Dil. Right—left ?

Mrs. B. The horses have escaped and a storm is rising. Oh dear, what will become of us ?

Dil. My dear Mrs. Billowby, don't trouble yourself about getting home. My cottage across the lake is entirely at your disposal. All are welcome there, yourself especially. The light of your beautiful countenance illuminating the portals of my humble cot would be like unto a momentary gleam of paradise.

Mrs. B. (*aside*). How divinely beautiful !

Dil. My dear **Mrs.** Billowby—may I say Anastasia ?—the rude and halting words of my poor tongue cannot fitly express the ideas which throng my teeming brain when I gaze upon your cameo face and fairy form.

Mrs. B. If I thought I could **trust** you—but alas ! you know that I am hampered with a large **fortune,** and men are prone to deceive.

Dil. Dissipate your fortune—throw it away, give it away—but don't let your miserable money bar **me** out. My admiration for you is above par, payable on demand. Join me, my dear Anastasia, and we'll form **a** joint **stock** company with unlimited liability to increase our numbers !

Mrs. B. Eh ?

Dil. In a moral way.

Mrs. B. How my heart flutters. But—but there is Mr. Chuggs—if I thought we could avoid him——

Dil. We **can**—we will ! Divine **Anastasia,** let's elope !

Mrs. B. When ?

Dil. Now. I'll take you across **the** lake and leave you in security. Then I'll send for the **others** and we'll **give** them the grandest surprise party of **the** year.

Mrs. B. How perfectly delightful ! I will be ready in a moment. *Fanny ready L. L E.* [**Exit** R. I E.

Dil. Tony, you're going it, you're **going** it. You always do go it, but this time—um—let me consider. I'll leave dearest Anastasia **at** the cottage, and have Tom set old Chuggs on her track. She will be frightened into fits and will marry him offhand. Then I'll have my platonic elopement with Effie and have some one post Tom after her. Meanwhile I'll run away with Fanny sure enough. There's diplomacy worthy of a Talleyrand. I say Tom—— *Mrs. Billowby ready R. I E.*

Enter TOM, L. I E., *with umbrella and wrap.*

Tom. Don't stop me, old fellow—I'm in a h-hurry.

Dil. You ?

Tom. Yes—I'm going to r-run away with Fanny.

Dil. You are, eh ?

Tom. You told me to m-make love to **her.**

Dil. But I did *not* tell you to go that far.

Tom. No—but I've g-gone.

Dil. Well, you haven't, and what is more **you** won't. You —a married man ! **You** should be ashamed of yourself.

Tom. Oh, bother ! Don't *you* preach.

Enter CHUGGS *and* PLUNKER, L. U. E., *with baskets.* TOM *joins them, all remaining up* L.

Dil. (*down* C.). Married **people** should never elope. The effect on society is very bad.

Enter FANNY, L. 2 E.

Fan. Tony !

Dil (*aside*). **Fanny !** The deuce !

Fan. I've got rid of Tom, (*runs to* DIL.) and now I'm all ready to run away with you !

All (*aside*). Run away with him !

Fan. Won't it be jolly !

Dil. Tremendously.

Chug. I say, Plunker—he-he ! *Your* Fanny—he-he——

Pl. Oh, dry up ! [FANNY *goes up* R.

Dil. (*aside*). Confound it, she has upset everything !

Effie ready L. 2 E.

Enter MRS. BILLOWBY, R. 1 E.

Ready for curtain

Broken glass ready R. U. E.

Mrs. B. Tony ! My dearest, dearest Tony ! (*Runs to him.*

All. *Her* dearest Tony !

Ch. Damn **her** dearest Tony !

Mrs. B. Are you all ready to elope with me ?

Fan. (*coming down*). Elope with *you ?* He's going to elope with *me*.

Mrs. B. No, he isn't !

Fan. Yes, he is !

Mrs. B. He isn't !

Fan. He is !

Tom. T-t-time !

Mrs. B. (R.). How's this, sir ? Speak, sir, speak !

Fan. (L.). Yes, how is it ? **Speak,** sir, speak !

All (*chorus*). Yes, sir ! Speak, **sir,** speak.

Dil. (C.). Merciful heavens ! You'd scarce expect one of my age to speak in public on the stage. If I should——

Fan. **Enough !** I'm done with you forever !

[*Paces stage excitedly, followed by* TOM *and* PLUNKER.

Mrs. B. Faithless trifler with my innocent, budding affections, be—gone ! [*Takes stage, followed by* CHUGGS.

Dil. (*stopping* TOM). My dear Tom, have you any message for your dear departed friends ? If so, speak, sir, speak, for I shall be a ghost in a couple of minutes. (TOM *breaks away. All go up except* DIL., *who goes* L.) I'll commit suicide, even though I lose my life. (*Recoils.*) Ah !

Enter EFFIE, L. 2 E.

Ef. (*runs to* DIL.). Now, Tony **dear,** I'm all ready.

All. *She's* all ready !

Pl. Egad, everybody's all ready !

Tom. Thunder and **lightning !** [*All pace stage.*

Dil.   Bury me under the weeping willows, and see that my grave's kept green !

     [*Stumbles against* CHUGGS, *who drops large basket* C., *into which* DIL. *falls.*

CURTAIN.

FOR SECOND CURTAIN, DIL. *is in basket, feet hanging out. The others are gathered around him shaking their fists and yelling,* "Speak, sir, speak."

QUICK CURTAIN.

ACT III.

ir has 2 cigars and matches.

Scene—*Same as Act I.   Discover* DIL. *asleep in easy chair up C., with handkerchief spread over his face.* TOM *is leaning over chair* L.   *Other characters ready to talk off R.*

Tom.   People may say what they please, but I am positive there never yet was a p-picnic that did not wind up in a storm, a fight, or a row of some sort.   Tony and I got home ahead of the others who are c-coming afoot.   Doesn't he t-take it coolly ? Sleeping as sound as the—er—unborn babe.   Tony !   T-Tony ! Wake up !

Dil.   Eh ? (*Yawns.*)   What's the row, Tom !   House afire ?

Tom.   N-no, the house isn't afire, but you will be under fire when the women arrive.

Dil.   That's so.   Three pair of angry eyes, backed by three angry tongues in active eruption, would vanquish a Napoleon. Tom, behold in me an awful warning.   Never, never try to elope with three women at once.

Tom.   No danger.   I found one a blame sight too many.

Dil.   Well, let's prepare for the fray.

Tom (*gloomily*).   I expect there will be a d-devil of a time.

     [*Sits* L.

Dil.   Nonsense.   Don't get a fit of the hypos.

Tom.   It's all right to t-talk.   Just wait until you have a wife to f-fly at you.

Dil.   Your wife can say nothing.   She agreed to elope with me.

Tom.   That's true.

Dil.   And so did her mother.

Tom.   But she didn't do it—c-confound the luck !

Dil. (*up* C.).   Here they come !   Now, Tom, brace up.

Tom (*goes* R.).   All right,

Dil.   Where are you going ?
Tom.   After a b-bracer !
Dil.   Here, I say !   [Exit R.
Ef. (*off* C.).   Oh, I'll find him, I'll find him !   *Tom ready*
Dil. (*runs* L.).   Good Lord, I'll not face them alone.   [Exit L.

Enter EFFIE, *excitedly*, C.   *Hopper rea*

Ef.   Oh, I never was so angry in all my life ! I have been
made a fool of. (*Sits* R.)   It's perfectly outrageous ! I'll not
endure it ! (*Walks about.*)   And my husband—was he a con-
federate ?   No—he hasn't sense enough to be a rogue.   But I
shall have revenge. *We* shall have revenge ! (*Goes* L. ; *calls.*)
Tom ! Where are you ? (*At* L. D.)   Tom ! Tom ! Where
can he be ? (*Crosses to* R. D.)   *Tom !*

Enter DIL., L.

Dil. (*aside*).   Hello ! Bombshell number one !   [Exit L.
Ef. (*at* R. D.).   Tom ! Thomas Picton ! *Thomas !*

Enter TOM, R.   *Hopper ready L.*

Tom.   Did you speak, my dear ?
Ef.   *Did* I speak ?   Thomas Picton, are you a man ?
Tom.   M-my dear—I—why, *you* ought not to——
Ef.   *Are* you a *man ?*
Tom.   Well—yes—I—I believe so.
Ef.   Then I would *be* a man.
Tom.   My dear, *you* might f-find that rather difficult.
Ef.   I want revenge !
Tom.   Heh ?
Ef.   I want *re-venge !*
Tom.   But *I* haven't g-got any.
Ef.   Doctor Dillington Hopper has insulted me.
Tom.   Yas ?
Ef.   Yes.   Aren't you boiling with indignation ?
Tom (*very quietly*).   Oh, c-certainly.   I'm a regular Vesuvius.
Ef.   Then call him out.
Tom.   Out where ?
Ef.   To fight.
Tom.   Not much.   He's a regular slugger.
Ef.   A duel, sir.
Tom.   Heh ?
Ef.   A duel with swords—great, big, long, sharp steel swords.
Tom.   Do you suppose I want to get j-jabbed all full of holes ?
Ef.   Then take pistols.
Tom.   Pistols ?   He is the best shot in New York, while I
c-couldn't hit the earth at two paces.
Ef.   Are you afraid ?

Tom. N-no—but I can't see the joke in having Tony kill *me* just because *you* are *m-mad* at him.

Ef. You coward! (*Follows him.*) Coward! Coward! *Coward!* I'll—I'll challenge him myself! [Exit, *angrily*, R.

Tom. That settles it. Poor Tony—he's dead and buried!

Enter DIL., L.

Dil. Tom, has the bombshell exploded?

Tom. Yas—run—you're dead and buried.

Dil. Oh, am I? Whereabouts?

Tom. Yas. Mrs. Picton is going to challenge you. Swords, pistols, guns, cannon, dynamite—the Lord knows what.

Dil. Mrs. Picton?

Tom. Yas. She wanted me to, but I c-couldn't see it.

Dil. You don't want me to kill you, I suppose?

Tom. I'm not especially anxious.

Dil. Then I have it—by Jove, I have it! You challenge me —we fight—that is, *I* fight. I take a pistol—I load it—I shoot you through the leg or the head or wherever you please. Do you see?

Tom. N-no—not exactly.

Dil. It's plain as a pikestaff. When Effie learns that you have risked your life for her, she will forgive *you*, because *she* tried to run away with *me*. See? You may lose a leg or perhaps your head, but never mind that. Get a wooden one.

[*Goes up.*

Tom. I'll be hanged if I——

Dil. Hush! I hear Anastasia's martial tread. Go and tell Effie that we're going to fight, and all that.

Tom. But I—— D-damn it, Tony, I don't see——

Dil. (*pushing him* R.). All right—very well—never mind— *get out!* (Exit TOM, R.) Whew! Now for bombshell number two. [Exit L.

Enter MRS. B., FANNY, CHUGGS *and* PLUNKER, C. *The ladies are both excited and angry.* FANNY *is at the* R. *of* MRS. B., CHUGGS *at* FANNY'S R., PLUNKER *at* MRS. B.'S L. FANNY *goes* R., *followed by* PLUNKER. MRS. B. *goes* L., *followed by* CHUGGS. *The men meet and collide at* C. *They draw up, glare, seek to pass, and again collide.*

Pl. Sir, you!

Ch. You, sir!

Pl. (*going* R.). My dear Mrs. Mayfair. [*She crosses to* L.

Ch. (*going* L. *at same time*). My dearest Anastasia.

[*She crosses to* R. *The men meet as before.*

Pl. Can't you see an inch from your nose?

Ch.   Oh, get out of my way, sir !   [*Follows* MRS. B. *up* R.

Pl.   My dear Mrs. Mayfair, I assure you——

Fan. (*grasps his wrist suddenly and brings him down* C.). Professor Plunker, I think you profess to admire me.

Pl.   Admire you ?   By yon high-arched heaven I swear——

Fan.   You declared that life without me would be a howling wilderness.

Pl.   Howling   wilderness—howling ?   By yon high-arched heaven——

Fan.   That you would *die* for one of my heavenly smiles.

Pl.   Die for a smile ?   By yon high-arched——

Fan. (*intensely*).   Did you mean it ?

Pl.   Did I mean it ?   By yon high——

Fan.   Then if you love me, call out Dillington Hopper.

Pl.   Eh ?   I don't quite——

Fan.   Call out Dillington Hopper, and shoot him on the spot !

Pl.   O Lord !

Fan.   Obey me, sir !

> [*Goes up* L.   PLUNKER *collapses and drops into
> tête-a-tête, back to audience.*

Mrs. B.   Don't you speak to me of calmness, Mr. Chuggs !

Ch.   But, my darling Anastasia, you can't mean it.

Mrs. B.   I do mean it.   Nothing but bl—ood can wipe out the insult.

Ch.   But, my darling Anastasia——

Mrs. B.   I want r-r-revenge !

Ch.   But, my darling——

Mrs. B.   Silence !   You've heard me speak !   My innocent, tender, trusting, loving heart has been trampled under foot by this Doctor Dillington Hopper.   Call him out and I am yours forever.   Crumly, dear Crumly, am I not worth fighting for ? If you lose an arm my own will encircle you.   If you lose a—— ahem !   [*Goes up, confused.*

Ch.   But my——

Mrs. B.   Enough !   Enough !   I am to be your wife, or I am not.   Do as I bid you, or get you to a nunnery.   Away !   [Exit R.

Enter TOM, *as if flung on by* MRS. B., R.

Ch. (*to* TOM).   Bid as I tell you, or get you to a nunnery, I say !   (TOM *looks dazed, wheels and* Exit, *sedately*, R.)   Perhaps Mrs. Mayfair is not so bloodthirsty.   Can I be of any service to you, my dear Mrs. Mayfair ?

Fan. (*brings him down* C. *intensely*).   Mr. Crumly Chuggs, you *can*.

Ch.   I shall be delighted to——

Fan.   Send Dillington Hopper to grass !

Ch.   I don't comprehend what——

3

Fan.   Fit him with a pair **of wings** !

Ch.   Grasshopper wings ?   **Jerusalem** !   [*Drops into chair* L.

Pl. (*looks around*).   Old Chuggs—he-he-he—old Chuggs will get killed twice !   [*Turns back*.

Ch. (*aside*).   There was a fool **in my family as soon as** I was born !   *Hopper ready L. with cigars and n*

Enter TOM, R.

Tom.   My dear Fanny, I hope I can——

Fan. (*grabs his wrist*).   Mr. Thomas Picton, you can !

Tom.   Moses !   They've *all* been—'ic—been b-bracing up !

Fan. (*brings* TOM *down* C.).   Listen !   (CHUGGS *and* PLUN-KER *scramble to their feet and go up* R. *and* L.)   Dillington Hopper **has most** shamefully insulted me by making love **to** your wife **and** her mother.   For their sake, for your sake, for my sake, demand instant satisfaction.   Shoot him once for them and twice for me.   [*Exit* R.

Tom.   M-Moses !   [*Goes up*.

Pl.   Well, **sir**, go ahead and **challenge** him.

Ch.   After you, sir.

Pl.   After me ?   And **leave you to marry the widow, eh ?**   If that isn't the most **terrific gall** !

Ch.   Gall, sir ?

Pl.   Yes, sir, gall, **sir**.

Ch.   **Don't** provoke me, sir, don't provoke me.   I am not to be **bullied, sir.**   I shall challenge this doctor, for I **am** no coward, sir, whatever you may be, sir.   No, sir.   I am an old, elderly, and somewhat aged man, sir, but beware, sir, be-ware.

                              [*Exit* C.

Tom.   He is g-going to challenge Tony !

Pl. (*bouncing up*).   Yes, **sir**, and so am I.   **It** shall never be said that I was outdone by such **an** antiquated dodo.   Not much !   I'll walk in gore—I'll wade in gore—I'll swim in gore ! My name is Napoleon Bonaparte Plunker, and—don't—you—for-get—it !   [*Exit, loftily*, C.

Tom (*quietly*).   I don't **care** what other people say, but *I* say a picnic plays the d-devil all around.

Enter DIL., L.

Dil.   Well, Tom, **is the** storm over ?

Tom.   Storm ?   It's n-nothing short of an earthquake.

Dil.   Wait a moment.   (*Lights cigar and sits across chair.*) Now go ahead.   I'm ready for anything.   Give me **all** the hor-rible details.   Remember, I haven't seen a Sunday paper in a week.

Tom (*solemnly*).   Tony, **we've got** to f-fight.

Dil.   Of **course**.   Proceed.

Tom. In earnest.

Dil. Correct. I shoot you in the leg or the head or somewhere. That's all settled. Proceed.

Tom. I'm not j-joking.

Dil. Well, in that case I suppose I must shoot you in some vital spot. Sorry, you know, but then, (*blows smoke*) *that's* all settled. Proceed.

Tom. Hang it all, Tony, Mrs. Mayfair means business.

Dil. Mrs. Mayfair?

Tom. Yas. She told me to shoot you twice.

Dil. Look here, Tom. I'm entirely willing to fill you with bullets in a friendly way. But if Mrs. Mayfair is interested in this matter, I shall be under the very painful necessity of chopping you into hash.

Tom. But I object to being h-hashed.

Dil. Objection overruled. Consider yourself mincemeat from this moment. Is that all? If so, we will commence operations. I have some good cigars and a couple of elegant pistols in my valise—hair triggers—saw grip—regular young cannon. I'll bring them down—we'll light our weeds and begin operations. Meet me here (*looks at watch*) in fifteen minutes.

Tom. You know I can't s-shoot.

Dil. Never mind that. You press the trigger—the pistol does the rest.

Tom. And what will you do?

Dil. Give you two shots to my one. That's fair enough.

Tom. Yas—it's f-fair enough; but I'd rather have one shot to your none. [Exit L.

Dil. No doubt he would. Some men are so infernally selfish.

Enter CHUGGS, C.

Ch. Doctor Dillington Hopper!

Dil. Mr. Crumly Chuggs.

Ch. I want to consult you on a very serious matter.

Dil. Very well. [*Takes* CHUGGS' *wrist; consults watch.*

Ch. What are you doing, sir?

Dil. Hem! Pulse irregular, temperature high, bile congested.

Ch. Eh?

Dil. Stomach weak, brain ditto, lungs unsound and liver knocked into a cocked hat. Bad case, bad case.

Ch. Sir! I——

Dil. Take a dozen blue pills, a pint of soothing syrup, trust to luck and make your will.

Ch. (*crosses*). Burr-r-r!

Dil. You're welcome. Don't thank me. It's all right.

Ch. But, sir—damme, sir—it's *not* all right. I object to such treatment.

Dil. Ah, then you prefer homœopathy. Very well. Take one pill, dissolve it in a barrel of water, and shake well before using. Dose, three drops in a pint of water.

Ch. I am not to be turned off with a jest. I am a man, sir, a man !

Dil. Are you ? Now who'd have thought it ?

Ch. In the name of Mrs. Billowby I demand satisfaction.

Dil. (*aside*). Egad ! I never thought of her. Very well, sir. Meet me here in fifteen minutes, and I will accommodate you. (CHUGGS *starts* L.) By the way, have you any particular choice ?

Ch. Particular choice ?

Dil. You see, if I blow your brains out it will make such a deuce of a mess. Therefore if you have no objections I will pot you in the body.

Ch. Thank you, but I——

Dil. Don't mention it. No trouble, I assure you.

Ch. Pot me in the body ! O Lord ! [Exit L.

Dil. I wonder whether Chuggs should be shot, or spanked and put to bed ?

Enter PLUNKER, hastily, C.

Pl. Doctor Hopper !

Dil. (*aside*). Hello ! Another one ! It's getting interesting.

Pl. Doctor Hopper, I am obliged to ask——

Dil. No use, sir, no use. I've no money to loan.

Pl. I want no money, sir. (*Pounds table.*) It is satisfaction that I want. (*Pounds table.*) Satisfaction, do you hear ?

Dil. When you get entirely through pounding the furniture perhaps you will explain the nature of your malady. Is it cucumbers ?

Pl. Cucumbers, sir ? No, sir. It's Mrs. Billowby.

Dil. Ah ! (*Aside.*) Two of them. Mrs. Billowby means business.

Pl. •And I likewise demand satisfaction, sir, in behalf of Mrs. Mayfair.

Dil. You do ? (*Aside.*) How bloodthirsty these widows are ! Very well. Meet me here (*looks at watch*) in ten minutes. (PLUNKER *goes* R.) I say, professor, have you made your will ?

Pl. My will ?

Dil. Good heavens, man ! Do you want your heirs to fight over your motor ? (PLUNKER *groans and exit* R.) This is getting decidedly interesting. Tom—Chuggs—Plunker. (*Counts off on fingers.*) If this continues I am liable to be quite busy. (*Lights cigar.*) Hello ! I nearly forgot. I have an engagement here (*looks at watch*) in ten minutes.

Enter EFFIE, R.

Ef.   Oh, doctor, is it all over ?

Dil. (L. C.).   My dear Effie——

Ef.   Where is he ?

Dil. (*solemnly*).   Let us hope for the best.

Ef.   You have killed him !   (*Sobs.*)   Oh-h !   I see it all, I see it all !   [*Drops into chair* L.

Dil.   I wonder why they always say that ?

Enter FANNY, C.

Fan. (*aside*).   There's the monster now.   You wretched man, have you killed them ?

Dil. (*aside*).   That settles it.   I'll send them to the realms above in (*looks at watch*) exactly eight minutes.

Fan.   Did you hear me, sir ?

Dil.   I beg your pardon ?

Enter MRS. BILLOWBY, *hurriedly*, C.

Mrs. B.   Where is he—oh, doctor—where is he ?

Dil.   My dear Mrs. Billowby, if you will kindly suggest which of the numerous " he's " you mean——

Mrs. B.   There is only one " he " to me—my own brave, noble, loyal Crumly.   Where is he ?

Dil.   My dear Mrs. Billowby, I regret——

Mrs. B. (*screams*),   Ah !   You've slain him !   I see it all !
                                                                    [*Sits* R.

Dil.   And now *she* sees it all !

Ef.   Tell me, tell me, where does he lie ?

All (*chorus*).   Yes, sir, where do they lie ?

Dil.   Ladies, if you will allow me to get a word in edgewise, crosswise, cornerwise or otherwise, I will say that nobody lies, at present. (*Aside.*)   Except myself.

All (*in chorus*).   Go on, go on.

Dil.   Your champions are writing their wills and ordering their coffins.   As soon as these cheerful details are finished, the shooting will begin.

Ef.   Oh !

Mrs. B.   Then it is not too late.   I will send for——

Dil. (*stopping her*).   One moment.   You will please send for nobody until I settle with the present crowd.   Then I will be at liberty to slaughter your other champions so long as the crop holds out.   [Exit L.

Fan.   Isn't it dreadful ?   [*Sits* R. *of table* L.

Mrs. B.   Awful !   [*Sits on tête-a-tête.*

Ef.   Horrible !   [*At table,* L.

Mrs. B.   Men are such savages.

Fan. *(half crying).* Why can't they be gentle and patient like ourselves ? We never quarrel—*do* we ?—nor get mad and fight—do we ?

Mrs. B. *(same bus.).* No, indeed ; we are just like d-doves.

Ef. *(same).* And yet you made them fi-fi-fight.

Mrs. B. I know it ; but I was no worse than you or Fanny.

Ef. Yes, you were.

Mrs. B. *(tartly).* No, I was not.

Fan. Oh, but you were. A person of your years and experience should have known better.

Mrs. B. Indeed! Then, madam, when you arrive at years of discretion—if ever you do—perhaps—*perhaps* you will know better than to elope with another woman's husband. [*Exit* R.

Fan. Oh, what a spiteful creature !

Ef. Fanny !

Fan. Effie !   [*They embrace.*

Ef. We won't quarrel, will we, dear ?

Fan. Never, never, never !

Ef. Poor Tom ! I must save him.

Fan. Poor Tony ! so must I. It's three to one against him.

Ef. Isn't there a law against duelling ?

Fan. I suppose so. There are laws against almost everything.

Ef. But I dare say you can't prevent a *doctor* from killing people.

Fan. I am afraid not, dear.

Ef. If this duel goes on I shall be a w-w-widow. *(Sobs.)* And I look just frightful in black.

Fan. I'm a widow already, and liable to remain one—thanks to you !

Ef. To me ? *(Straightens up.)* Well, of all things ! I am sure that you were wickeder than I.

Fan. You forced Tom to fight.

Ef. Because you tried to run away with him.

Fan. And you endeavored to elope with Tony.

Ef. Ugh ! I've no patience with you ! [*Flounces out* R.

Fan. *(surprised).* Moral : In future my dear Fanny, you will take no part in family rows ; and you will shun picnic parties as you would a rattlesnake. Where shall I find those ferocious men ? *(At* C. D.*)* This duel must be stopped. If Tony Hopper gets killed, I'll never forgive him so long as I live !   [*Exit* C.

Enter DIL. and TOM, L., with three pistols.

Tom. I s-say, Tony, you're dead sure that these cannon aren't loaded ?

Dil. My dear Tom, I am surprised at you. The gun that

isn't loaded always kills. These pistols contain just enough powder to make a devil of a fizz !—bang !

> [*Swings pistol* L., *as* CHUGGS *and* PLUNKER **enter** ;
> *they* exeunt, *tumbling over each other.*

Tom. You scared the m-mummies.

Dil. Never mind them. Now for business. [*Up* L. C.

Tom (R. *front*). All right—blaze away.

D.l. All ready ?

Tom. Yas. [*Shuts eyes and turns head* **away.**

Dil. Open your eyes ! Now, one—two——

> [Enter EFFIE, *quickly*, C. *She screams, runs to* DIL. **and**
> *throws her arms around his neck.*

Ef. Spare him, spare him, he is my husband.

Tom. (*aside*). D-damn the luck !

Ef. Kill your patients, doctor, but please don't kill my Tom. (*Looks around.*) Oh, Tom, say you forgive me.

Dil. (*still embracing* EFFIE). Yes, Thomas, you better forgive her.

Tom (*drily*). Well, whenever you get entirely through your h-hugging match, you might release her, and I'll consider it.

Ef. (*still clinging to* DIL.). Yes, doctor, please release me and he will consider it.

Tom. Wait a minute. Will you induce your mother to m-marry old C-Chuggs ?

Ef. Yes.

Tom. And live by themselves ?

Ef. Oh, I can't promise that.

Dil. Very well, Tom, very well. (*They aim pistols as before.*) One—two——

Ef. Oh, yes, yes—I promise.

Tom. Then I forgive you. [*Embrace.*

Dil. Bless you, my children, bless you. Now get out, get out. (*Bundles them off* R.). Victory number one. Now for the others. (**Enter** CHUGGS *and* PLUNKER, L.) Gentlemen, you are late. However, as it will never happen again, I'll excuse you. Besides, I had some trouble with Tom. He died hard.

Ch. Died hard ?

Dil. Very hard.

Pl. I heard nothing.

Dil. Because I use a new and wonderful powder—an invention of my own. It is entirely noiseless, creates no smoke, and has ten times the power of any known explosive. Why, gentlemen, you will find it a positive luxury.

Ch. I dare say.

Dil. Some preliminaries are necessary before you shuffle

off this mortal coil. For one thing, your burial certificates must be filled out.

Pl. Burial certificate ?

Dil. Why, to be sure. You wouldn't die like paupers, would you ? Besides, the law requires that we turn men over to the undertaker in regular form. (*Takes out memo book and pencil.*) Now then—attention, please. You will solemnly state whether you are male or female ; black, white or colored ; age, height and weight ; are you tramps, paupers, idiots, anarchists, criminals, millionaires, Republicans, Democrats or Presbyterians ? Do you eat with a knife, chew gum, play the violin or smoke cigarettes ? And, finally, the cause of death. I believe, in the present case, that Mrs. Billowby is the exciting cause—am I right ?

Pl. Mrs. Billowby certainly *did* commission me to——

Ch. Beg your pardon, sir, but she commissioned *me*.

Pl. I beg *your* pardon, but Mrs. Billowby is a lady of taste, sir, and she promised me her hand if I challenged the doctor.

Ch. Promised *you*, sir ? She promised *me*.

Pl. It's false, you old sag-wap !

Ch. You're another, you old—old——

Dil. Gentlemen, gentlemen, this won't do. You came here to fight me, but I judge you are not only willing but anxious to fight each other.

Ch. *and* **Pl.** Yes, *sir !*

Dil. Then what do you say to a triangular duel ?

Ch. I never heard of a triangular duel.

Dil. It's very simple. You take this pistol and stand over there. (CHUGGS *goes to* L. *front.*) And you take this and stand there. (PLUNKER *at* R. *front.*) I will stand here. (*Up* C.) Now then, we are all ready. When I count three, I will chug Mr. Chuggs, and Mr. Chuggs can plunk Mr. Plunker.

Ch. But I don't want to be chugged.

Pl. And I'm not going to be plunkered !

Dil. Gentlemen, it is the only possible way. All ready. Aim ! (CHUGGS *aims over* PLUNKER'S *head.*) Good heavens, Chuggs ! Our friend Plunker is not eleven feet tall. Come down. Once more. All ready—aim ! (CHUGGS *holds arm before face and swings his pistol towards* R. E.) One—two——

MRS. B. *screams and* **enters** R.

Mrs. B. Murder ! Don't shoot me !

Dil. Recover arms.

Mrs. B. Crumly, dear Crumly, can you ever forgive me ?

Dil. Certainly he can. Haven't you saved his life ? In

another minute **he'd** have been scared to death.   Run to your
Chuggy !   [*She crosses to* CHUGGS.
   Pl.   Another **speculat**ion gone **to** smash.

Enter FANNY, TOM *and* EFFIE, C.

   Fan.   Not killed **?**   Oh, Tony !
   Dil. (C.).   **Fanny** !   [*They embrace.*
   Tom (R. **C.**).   Effie !   [*Embrace.*
   Mrs. B. (**L.**).   Oh, Chuggy !   [*Embrace.*
   Pl. (R.).   **Oh,** Plunker !   [*Embraces himself.*
   Tom.   I say, **Tony, you'll have a** story for the boys when you
get back into Wall Street.
   All.   Wall Street !
   Mrs. B.   Merciful **heavens ! Isn't he** a doctor ?
   Tom.   Yes—he **often doses** the market.
   Dil. (**to** MRS. B.).   And yesterday **I was at** least a doctor of
divinity.
   Mrs. B. (*coyly*).   Oh, Mr. Hopper.
   Tom.   M-Moses !
   Fan.   Perhaps, **Tony** dear, you can give us a final prescrip-
tion that will apply **to** everybody.
   Dil.   Well, I'll **try.**   (*To audience.*)   Ladies and gentlemen,
—Follow the Golden Rule **: Be** virtuous—in a moral way—
and **you** will all be happy.

CURTAIN.

A GILDED YOUTH.

A COMEDY IN THREE ACTS.

By CHARLES TOWNSEND.

Originally produced under the title of "Moses." Three male, two female characters. Scenery, three easy interiors; cotsumes, modern. This piece, originally produced by the author and employed by him for several seasons as part of his repertoire, provides for a full evening's entertainment and yet calls for but five characters. It is unique in this particular, and meets a want often felt by small professional companies as well as by amateurs. It naturally follows that every part is an important one, since so few people are required to carry the interest of the piece, which is second to none of the author's extensive list, and possesses to the full those qualities of briskness, bustle, wit, humor, and "go" which constitute his professional trademark. Its story is necessarily a slender one, but it is complicated with an unusual wealth of humorous incident and ludicrous situation, and its action never flags for an instant. An "all star" comedy for low comedian, "touch and go" light comedian, old man, old maid, and soubrette. Strongly recommended.

Price . . . . 25 Cents.

SYNOPSIS.

ACT I.—Time, a midsummer afternoon. Long Branch. A romantic maiden. The Colonel gets news. Sam and Sadie. The pitcher of milk and the tale of a cat. Aunt Sadie's "nerves." Moses! A case of mix. Sam gains a promise. Trouble threatened Trouble comes. A grand smash.

ACT II.— Five minutes later. Sam's letter. Law and love. Sadie's suggestions. The "Slugger." Sam on his muscle. Moses and the Colonel. More mistakes. "Settled out of court." The broken promise. Moses a wreck. "I want revenge." A joint-stock love-letter. Sam's device. Aunt Sadie sees a chance at last. Sam reads the Riot Act. Comical climax.

ACT III.—An hour later. At the Colonel's. Aunt Sadie grows impatient. Moses more mystified. Sam talks politics with the usual result. The Colonel on the warpath. Sadie's scheme. "Back me up now." The storm approaches. A cyclone — of fun. Sam's triumph. "After the storm, a calm."

APOLLO'S ORACLE.

By ESTHER B. TIFFANY.

An entertainment in one act. This novel entertainment is admirably adapted for summer theatricals at hotels or country-houses, not only because it requires no scenery and calls for Greek costumes only, which are easily arranged, but because its fun depends as much upon the audience as upon the actors. Two ladies and one boy are required for its representation, and any number of girls for chorus. Complete with music.

Price . . . . 15 Cents

New Hampshire Gold.

A COMEDY-DRAMA IN THREE ACTS.

By KATHERINE E. RAND.

Eight male, six female characters. Scenery easily arranged; costumes, modern. An excellent piece, interesting in story, and full of shrewd and humorous character. It has a strong melodramatic interest, but its general atmosphere is homely and domestic, placing it in the class of plays to which "The Old Homestead" belongs. It provides some capital parts, both serious and humorous, and is well suited for the simplest conditions under which amateur theatricals are given. Printed from an acting copy which has been successfully performed. Plays two hours.

Price, ... 15 Cents.

SYNOPSIS.

ACT I. At the Gerrishes. The thirst of gold. "A poor fool." David and Daisy. Lessons in flirtation. The laziest man on the farm. Putting out the fire. The landslide. The speculator from Boston. An old fox. The gold mine. "I'm determined to marry a very rich man." The partnership. David's refusal.

ACT II. The mortgage. Christie's misgivings. Salting the mine. The lost letter. "The Boston feller." Mandy's paper dolly. A clue. To the mine. "Whatever it is, Christie Gerrish is goin' to be in 't." Caught in the act. Dissembling. The speculator's revenge. Daisy's interrupted vow. The awful tidings. Daisy true gold. "I don't care if it's ten thousand nights; let me go, mother, let me go!"

ACT III. The dead speculator. The convalescent. "As cross as two sticks." A lost memory. Jack and Daisy. A misunderstanding. The Colonel's daughter. "That letter." Gid and Bijah. A thunderstorm, which clears the air. The crisis. David's sacrifice. "I've never been able to remember anything about it." The mortgage. The debt paid. "I am the richest man in the world."

A Tell=Tale Eyebrow.

A COMEDY IN TWO ACTS.

By ESTHER B. TIFFANY.

Author of "A RICE PUDDING," "A MODEL LOVER," ETC.

Two male, four female characters. Scenery, an easy interior; costumes, modern and elegant. A very pretty and graceful little piece of healthy sentiment and refined humor, perfectly adapted for amateur performers and appealing to the best taste in such matters. In story and treatment alike this latest piece is agreeably characteristic of the author of "A Rice Pudding," and can hardly fail to please the taste to which that popular piece so successfully appealed. Plays an hour and a quarter.

Price, ... 15 Cents.

Broken Bonds.

A DRAMA IN FOUR ACTS.

By F. E. HILAND.

Author of "ROONEY'S RESTAURANT," "A TOWN MEETING,"
"THE OLD COUNTRY STORE," ETC.

Nine male, three female characters. Costumes, modern and rough Western; scenery, varied, but not difficult. This is a stirring melodrama of the conventional type, but not lacking in originality and novelty of story, incident, and character. Its action is rapid and exciting, its dialogue vigorous and forcible, its comedy element natural and sympathetic, its serious interest strong and absorbing. It provides several good, heavy parts, and excellent low comedy, Negro and Yankee, and gives plenty of chances for strong acting. Plays two hours.

Price, ... **15 Cents.**

SYNOPSIS.

ACT I. SCENE 1.—Wilke's new quarters. Bill and Joe concoct a scheme to rob Richard. "That's the stuff to drive dull care away." Playing for high stakes. "My money gone." The midnight murder. "I'll fasten this on that sot there." The stricken wife. Richard's vow. "Till then I am dead to all I hold dear on earth."

ACT II. SCENE 1.—Fifteen years after. The mountain home. Deacon Gimp and his trials. A war cloud on the horizon. SCENE 2.—Sam's soliloquy. "Oh, you old reptile, I see yer game!" Wilke makes a discovery. SCENE 3.—The forsaken wife. "Fifteen years and nothing heard from my poor husband." Clara's loss. The villain's letter. "Heaven help you if you are dependent upon that man!" Wilke's revelation. "A slave, would that I never was born!"

ACT III. SCENE 1.—War at last. Edward's despair. "Chained at home." Gimp's grip. Sam to the rescue. "Take it, you old blood-sucker!" SCENE 2.—The villain's lair. Edward attempts a rescue. Pete puts him on the right track. Wilke has an unwelcome visitor. His schemes frustrated. Clara's misery. A friend in need. "That gal's goin' long o' us." SCENE 3.—Down by the river. Wilke wiles Sam's big fish. "What shall I dew with the critter?" Clara's escape. "Yer slave is free!" Tableau: Crossing the river.

ACT IV. SCENE 1.—Sam and Pete happy. Father and Son. Wilke jubilant. "The game is about to fall into my snare." SCENE 2.—The loved ones at home. Arrival of Edward and Sam. Sam's stranger. "He's not what he seems." Wilke plays his trump card. Ward as a witness. "You are innocent." Happy finale. "We will cast aside our broken bonds." Grand Tableau.—Victory's Crown.

A Change of Color.

A PLAY IN ONE ACT.

By CLARA J. DENTON.

Author of "THE MAN WHO WENT TO EUROPE," "TO MEET MR. THOMPSON," etc.

Two male, three female characters. Scenery and costumes unimportant. A little dramatic trifle for school or parlor. Plays fifteen minutes.

Price, ... **15 Cents.**